Also by Rachael Reed

Codefendant

Codefendant

Once a Cheater

Once a Cheater

Passport Bro

What Happens in Prison

Preference

Sprinkle Sprinkle

Championship Bad

Street Exodus

Street Exodus

Street Royalty

Pawns of Power

SIS

Cartel Bloodline

Get Money Girls

Skip the Games

Til Death Do Us Part

Backpage Hustle

Link in Bio

The Virgin and The Kingpin

The Virgin and a Kingpin

Rachael Reed
©2024

The Virgin and a Kingpin

By Rachael Reed

Copyright © 2024 by Rachael Reed

Check Out More Great Products and Free Giveaways

https://tbdbpublishing.com/

Chapter 1: Flights to Paradise

Megan sat in the cramped airplane seat, her nerves jittery from a mix of excitement and exhaustion. She leaned her head back against the seat, trying to push the stress of her demanding job out of her mind. It had been a relentless few months at the firm, and this vacation with her best friend Lila was supposed to be her escape from the suffocating grip of deadlines and demanding clients.

Lila, her energetic and spontaneous counterpart, was practically bouncing in her seat beside her. "Girl, we are gonna tear Cancun up! No more emails, no more bosses, just sun, sand, and fine men!"

Megan laughed, her tension easing slightly. "I'm just looking forward to some peace and quiet. Maybe a good book and a few margaritas."

Lila rolled her eyes. "You need to loosen up, Meg. This trip is about letting go. You work too damn hard."

Megan nodded, knowing Lila was right. She had been living life in the fast lane, chasing career goals with blinders on. This vacation was a chance to breathe, to find herself again. As the plane began its descent, Megan felt a flicker of excitement. Maybe, just maybe, she could find a bit of adventure.

On the other side of the plane, Jerel Phillips stared out the window, his thoughts a mix of business and pleasure. He was headed to Cancun under the guise of a vacation, but the trip had another purpose. Meetings with suppliers and competitors were scheduled, but he planned to enjoy the luxuries that the tropical paradise had to offer. Jerel, known as "JP" in the streets, was a man who had climbed to the top of the drug game through charm, intelligence, and ruthlessness.

Dre, his right-hand man, leaned over. "We good for tonight, JP. The Colombians are ready to talk."

Jerel nodded, a smirk playing on his lips. "Good. But let's not forget to enjoy ourselves. We're in paradise, after all."

Dre chuckled. "You got it, boss. But keep your eyes open. This place might be paradise, but it's still dangerous."

Jerel's gaze swept over the cabin, his eyes narrowing on the passengers. His life had taught him to always be alert, to never let his guard down. As the plane touched down and passengers began to disembark, he felt a rush of anticipation. Cancun was a playground, and he intended to make the most of it.

The humid air hit Megan like a wall as she stepped off the plane. She took a deep breath, savoring the salty tang of the ocean breeze. "This is it, Lila. Our adventure begins now."

Lila grinned, pulling out her phone to take a selfie. "To the best vacation ever!"

They collected their bags and caught a taxi to their resort, the vibrant streets of Cancun whizzing past in a blur of color and sound. Megan felt a thrill of excitement. The resort was everything they had hoped for – white sandy beaches, crystal clear pools, and an endless supply of tropical drinks.

As they checked in, the receptionist handed them two key cards. "Welcome, ladies. You're in for a treat. Enjoy your stay."

Megan couldn't help but smile. "I think I will."

Jerel's arrival at his luxury villa was met with a flurry of activity. Security personnel buzzed around, ensuring everything was in place. Jerel walked through the spacious living area, admiring the view of the ocean from the floor-to-ceiling windows. This was a far cry from the gritty streets he controlled back home.

Dre set down their bags. "This place is tight, JP. You gonna be able to relax?"

Jerel chuckled, his eyes scanning the horizon. "For a bit, maybe. But we got business to handle first."

The villa was equipped with everything they needed, including a private pool and a fully stocked bar. Jerel poured himself a drink, savoring the moment of calm. But his mind was already calculating, planning the meetings and negotiations that lay ahead.

That evening, Megan and Lila hit the resort's beachside bar, the sound of waves crashing against the shore creating a soothing backdrop. Megan sipped her margarita, letting the alcohol warm her from the inside out. Lila was already on the dance floor, flirting with a group of guys. Megan laughed, shaking her head. Lila was in her element.

As she watched the sunset, Megan felt a presence beside her. She turned to see a tall, handsome man with an air of confidence that bordered on arrogance. "Mind if I join you?"

Megan's heart skipped a beat. "Sure, go ahead."

"I'm Jerel," he said, extending a hand. "Here on vacation?"

Megan took his hand, feeling a jolt of electricity. "Megan. And yes, just trying to relax and forget about work for a while."

Jerel smiled, his eyes dark and intense. "Sounds like a good plan. Mind if I keep you company?"

Megan felt a flutter of nerves. "Not at all."

They talked as the sky turned from orange to deep blue, the chemistry between them undeniable. Megan found herself drawn to Jerel, his confidence and charm intoxicating. She was intrigued by the mystery that seemed to surround him, unaware of the dangerous world he was a part of.

As the night deepened, Jerel couldn't shake the feeling that meeting Megan was a twist of fate. She was different from the women he usually encountered – intelligent, genuine, and completely unaware of his dark side. It was refreshing, and he found himself wanting to know more about her.

But as they laughed and talked, the realities of their worlds loomed over them like dark clouds. Jerel knew he couldn't hide his true self forever, and Megan's innocence made him want to protect her from the dangers he faced daily.

Chapter 2: Serendipity

The beach party was in full swing, the rhythmic beats of reggaeton pulsing through the humid night air. Megan stood at the edge of the crowd, sipping her drink and watching the waves crash against the shore. Lila was somewhere in the throng, dancing and flirting without a care in the world. Megan felt a pang of envy. She wished she could be that carefree, but her mind was still back home, tangled in the stress of her job.

"Hey, you look like you could use another drink," a deep voice cut through the music. Megan turned to see Jerel, the man she had met at the bar earlier. His presence was magnetic, his confidence palpable.

She smiled, feeling a spark of excitement. "Why not? I'm here to have fun, after all."

Jerel handed her a fresh cocktail, his fingers brushing hers. The electricity between them was undeniable. "So, Megan, what brings you to Cancun?"

Megan took a sip, the alcohol warming her insides. "Just needed a break. Work's been crazy, and I needed to get away. What about you?"

Jerel's eyes darkened slightly, but his smile remained. "Business and pleasure. Mostly pleasure, I hope."

Megan raised an eyebrow. "What kind of business?"

Jerel shrugged, taking a long drink. "Let's just say it's complicated. But enough about that. What do you do?"

"I'm a lawyer," Megan replied, feeling a bit self-conscious. "I know, boring, right?"

Jerel laughed, the sound rich and warm. "Not boring at all. I respect that. Takes a lot of brains and guts."

Their conversation flowed effortlessly, each word drawing them closer. Megan felt herself relaxing, the tension melting away. Jerel was different from anyone she had ever met. He was confident, charming, and there was an edge to him that intrigued her.

Meanwhile, the party raged on around them. The music thumped, bodies moved in rhythm, and laughter filled the air. But for Megan and Jerel, it was as if they were in their own world. They found a quieter spot on the beach, the sounds of the party fading into the background.

Jerel looked out at the ocean, his expression contemplative. "You ever feel like you're living two lives?"

Megan nodded, understanding the sentiment all too well. "Every day. The person I am at work and the person I am with my friends... sometimes it's hard to reconcile the two."

Jerel's gaze was intense as he looked at her. "I get that. I've got a life back home that's... complicated. But here, with you, it feels simple."

Megan's heart raced. She barely knew this man, yet she felt a connection to him that she couldn't explain. "Tell me more about you, Jerel. The real you."

Jerel hesitated, then sighed. "I grew up in a tough neighborhood. Made some choices to survive. Now, I run things. It's not an easy life, but it's mine."

Megan could see the pain behind his eyes, the weight of his past. She reached out, touching his arm gently. "We all have our battles. What matters is who we choose to be now."

Jerel smiled, his gaze softening. "You're something else, Megan. Most people don't get that."

As the night went on, their conversation grew deeper, more personal. Megan shared stories of her childhood, her struggles with balancing career and personal life. Jerel listened, genuinely interested. He found himself opening up to her in ways he hadn't with anyone else.

The chemistry between them was undeniable. Megan found herself drawn to Jerel, his confidence, his vulnerability. It was a dangerous attraction, but she couldn't resist. They walked along the beach, the moonlight casting a silvery glow on the water.

Jerel stopped, turning to face her. "Megan, I know we just met, but I feel like there's something here. Something real."

Megan's heart pounded in her chest. She felt the same way, but it scared her. "I feel it too, Jerel. But it seems our worlds are so different."

Jerel stepped closer, his eyes locked on hers. "Sometimes, different is good. Sometimes, it's what we need."

The air between them crackled with tension. Megan could feel his breath on her skin, the heat radiating from his body. She knew this was crazy, but she didn't care. She wanted him, needed him.

Jerel leaned in, his lips brushing hers. The kiss was slow, tender, filled with a promise of more to come. Megan melted into him, her arms wrapping around his neck. She had never felt this way before, never experienced a kiss that made her whole body tingle.

The night continued, each moment drawing them closer. They danced, laughed, and shared more about their lives. Megan felt like she was falling into a dream, one she never wanted to end. Jerel was intoxicating, and she couldn't get enough.

As the party began to wind down, they found themselves back at the resort, the night air cool and refreshing. Jerel walked Megan to her room, their hands intertwined. "I had an amazing time tonight, Megan."

Megan smiled, her heart full. "Me too, Jerel. Thank you for everything."

Jerel leaned in, kissing her softly. "Goodnight, beautiful. I'll see you tomorrow."

Megan watched him walk away, her mind spinning with the possibilities. She knew this was just the beginning, and she couldn't wait to see where it would lead.

Chapter 3: Building a Connection

The next few days in Cancun felt like a dream to Megan. Each morning, she woke up with a sense of anticipation, knowing that she would spend the day with Jerel. He was a puzzle she wanted to solve, a dark, mysterious man who made her feel alive in ways she had never imagined. They spent their days exploring the island, and each adventure brought them closer.

On the second morning, Jerel picked Megan up from her resort in a sleek, black convertible. As they cruised down the coast, the wind whipping through their hair, Megan couldn't help but feel a rush of excitement.

"Where we headed today?" Megan asked, her voice tinged with curiosity.

Jerel flashed her a smile, his eyes hidden behind dark sunglasses. "Thought we'd check out some of the local spots. Get a real taste of Cancun."

Their first stop was a bustling market filled with vibrant colors and intoxicating smells. Jerel guided Megan through the narrow aisles, pointing out various trinkets and local delicacies. Megan found herself captivated by his knowledge and the ease with which he navigated the crowded space. It was clear he was no stranger to places like this, and she felt safe with him by her side.

"Ever try tamales?" Jerel asked, handing her a steaming corn husk.

Megan shook her head, her eyes wide with anticipation. "No, but I'm game."

Jerel watched with a grin as she took her first bite, her eyes lighting up with delight. "These are amazing!"

"There's a lot more where that came from," Jerel replied, his voice low and enticing.

As the day wore on, they continued their exploration, visiting hidden beaches and ancient ruins. Jerel seemed to know all the best spots, and

Megan felt like she was seeing a side of Cancun she never would have found on her own. They talked about everything and nothing, sharing stories from their pasts and dreams for the future. Megan found herself opening up to Jerel in ways she never had with anyone else.

At a secluded beach, they sat side by side on a large rock, the waves crashing around them. Megan stared out at the horizon, her thoughts swirling. "You know, I never expected to meet someone like you here."

Jerel glanced at her, his expression unreadable. "Same here. You're different, Megan. In a good way."

Megan smiled, feeling a warmth spread through her. "You make me feel... alive."

Jerel's eyes softened. "You are alive, Megan. Don't let life pass you by."

As the sun set, they found themselves at a small, rustic restaurant overlooking the ocean. The atmosphere was intimate, the candlelight casting a warm glow over their faces. Megan felt a flutter in her chest as Jerel reached across the table, taking her hand in his.

"I've been thinking," he said, his voice serious. "We come from different worlds, but I feel something real with you."

Megan's heart raced. "I feel it too, Jerel. But your world... it scares me."

Jerel's grip tightened on her hand. "I know. And I won't lie to you – it's dangerous. But I want to protect you from that. I want you in my life, Megan."

Megan looked into his eyes, seeing the sincerity there. She knew this was crazy, but she couldn't deny her feelings. "I want that too, Jerel. But how do we make it work?"

Jerel leaned in, his gaze intense. "We'll figure it out, one step at a time."

The next few days passed in a blur of passion and connection. Megan felt herself falling deeper for Jerel, each moment with him intensifying her feelings. They shared their fears and hopes, their conversations deep and meaningful. Megan had never felt so understood, so seen.

One night, as they lay on the beach under a blanket of stars, Megan turned to Jerel, her heart pounding. "Tell me something real, Jerel. Something you've never told anyone."

Jerel was silent for a moment, his eyes fixed on the sky. "I've done things I'm not proud of, Megan. Things that haunt me. But being with you... it makes me want to be better."

Megan felt tears prick her eyes. "You can be better, Jerel. We all have a past, but it doesn't define us."

Jerel turned to her, his expression raw. "You're the best thing that's ever happened to me, Megan. I don't want to lose you."

"You won't," Megan whispered, leaning in to kiss him. The kiss was tender, filled with unspoken promises and a deep, unyielding connection.

Their days together were magical, but the reality of their lives loomed over them like a dark cloud. Megan knew their time in paradise was limited, but she chose to focus on the present, savoring every moment with Jerel. She had never felt so alive, so free.

As the days were winding down and their final day approached, Megan's heart ached with the thought of leaving Jerel. They had built something real, something beautiful, and the idea of returning to her old life without him was unbearable.

Chapter 4: Romantic Escapades

The sun dipped low in the Cancun sky, casting a warm, golden hue over the city. Megan and Jerel strolled hand in hand along the beach, the soft sand cushioning their steps. The past few days had been a whirlwind of emotions and discoveries, and tonight, Jerel had something special planned.

"Where we goin'?" Megan asked, her curiosity piqued as they walked away from the bustling resort.

Jerel grinned, his eyes sparkling with mischief. "You'll see. Just trust me."

They continued down the beach until they reached a secluded spot. A small table set for two awaited them, illuminated by the soft glow of lanterns hanging from nearby palm trees. The sound of the waves provided a soothing backdrop, creating an atmosphere of intimacy and romance.

Megan's breath caught in her throat. "Jerel, this is beautiful."

Jerel pulled out a chair for her, his touch lingering on her back. "Only the best for you, Megan."

They sat down, and a waiter appeared, serving them a sumptuous meal of fresh seafood and tropical fruits. As they ate, they talked about everything and nothing, their connection growing deeper with each passing moment.

Megan found herself opening up to Jerel in ways she never had with anyone else. She shared her dreams, her fears, and the pressures of her job. Jerel listened intently, his eyes never leaving her face.

"You're amazing, you know that?" Jerel said, his voice low and sincere. "Smart, beautiful, and strong. Don't let anyone tell you otherwise."

Megan blushed, feeling a warmth spread through her. "You're not so bad yourself, Mr. Phillips. You've got layers."

Jerel chuckled, leaning back in his chair. "More than you'll ever know."

After dinner, Jerel led Megan to a clearing where a small, makeshift dance floor had been set up. The lanterns cast a soft glow over the area, creating an enchanting ambiance. Jerel took Megan's hand, pulling her close as a slow, sultry song began to play.

"Dance with me," he murmured, his breath hot against her ear.

Megan melted into his embrace, their bodies moving in perfect harmony. She could feel the heat radiating from him, the raw energy of his presence overwhelming her senses. They swayed to the rhythm of the music, lost in their own world.

Jerel's hand slid down to the small of her back, pulling her even closer. Megan's heart pounded in her chest, her breath coming in shallow gasps. She looked up into his eyes, seeing the desire mirrored in his gaze.

"Jerel..." she whispered, her voice trembling.

He leaned down, his lips brushing against hers in a feather-light touch. The kiss was tentative at first, but quickly deepened into something more intense. Megan's hands tangled in his hair, pulling him closer as their kiss ignited a fire within her.

It was her first real kiss, and it was everything she had imagined and more. Jerel's lips were firm yet gentle, his touch both possessive and tender. She felt a rush of emotions – desire, passion, and a deep, aching need.

Jerel pulled back slightly, his eyes dark with longing. "You okay, baby?"

Megan nodded, her voice barely a whisper. "More than okay."

The night continued with more dancing, more kisses, and more shared secrets. Megan felt like she was floating on a cloud, her worries and fears melting away in Jerel's arms. He made her feel alive, cherished, and desired in ways she had never experienced before.

As the night drew to a close, Jerel walked Megan back to her room. They stood outside her door, the weight of the evening settling over them.

"I had an amazing time tonight," Megan said, her voice filled with emotion. "Thank you, Jerel."

Jerel cupped her face in his hands, his touch sending shivers down her spine. "The pleasure was all mine, Megan. You make me wanna be a better man."

Megan's heart swelled with emotion. "You already are, Jerel. You just have to believe it."

He leaned down, kissing her softly one last time. "Goodnight, beautiful."

"Goodnight," Megan whispered, watching as he walked away. She felt a mix of emotions – joy, longing, and a hint of sadness. She knew their time together was limited, but she was determined to make the most of it.

The next few days were a whirlwind of romantic escapades. They explored hidden coves, snorkeled in crystal-clear waters, and shared intimate dinners under the stars. Each moment was filled with laughter, passion, and a growing sense of connection.

Megan found herself falling deeper for Jerel, her feelings for him intensifying with each passing day. He was unlike anyone she had ever known – strong, protective, and deeply caring. Despite the danger that surrounded him, she felt safe in his presence.

But as their vacation drew to a close, the reality of their separate worlds loomed over them like a dark cloud. Megan knew that their time in paradise was coming to an end, and the thought of returning to her old life without Jerel was unbearable.

Chapter 5: Deepening Bonds

The sun blazed high in the Cancun sky as Megan and Jerel strolled hand-in-hand down the busy market street. Vendors called out to them, selling everything from handmade jewelry to fragrant spices. Megan's senses were on overload, but she felt more alive than ever.

"Check this out," Jerel said, guiding her to a stall filled with vibrant tapestries. "You ever seen something this colorful?"

Megan shook her head, her eyes wide with wonder. "It's beautiful. Everything here is."

Jerel watched her, a soft smile on his lips. "Not as beautiful as you."

Megan blushed, playfully shoving him. "You're too smooth, Jerel."

"Only for you, baby."

They spent the morning exploring the market, tasting exotic fruits and haggling with the vendors. Megan felt a freedom she hadn't experienced in years, a lightness that came from living in the moment. With Jerel by her side, she was able to forget about the pressures of her life back home.

By afternoon, they found themselves on a secluded beach, the turquoise waters inviting them for a swim. Jerel stripped down to his shorts, revealing a body covered in tattoos, each one telling a story of his life. Megan admired the artistry, intrigued by the man behind the ink.

"Come on in, the water's perfect," Jerel called out, splashing playfully.

Megan hesitated for a moment before joining him, the cool water washing away her reservations. They swam and played, their laughter echoing across the empty beach. Jerel pulled her close, his hands strong and steady.

"You're something else, Megan," he murmured, his lips brushing against her ear.

Megan felt a shiver run down her spine. "You make me feel alive, Jerel. Like I can do anything."

Jerel's eyes darkened with intensity. "You can, baby. You're stronger than you know."

They spent hours in the water, sharing stories and secrets, their connection deepening with each passing moment. Megan found herself falling harder for Jerel, her feelings intensifying as they grew closer.

That evening, they returned to their favorite spot on the beach, a small fire pit casting a warm glow over the sand. They sat close together, wrapped in a blanket, watching the flames dance. The night air was filled with the sounds of the ocean and the distant hum of nightlife.

"Tell me something real, Jerel," Megan said softly, her head resting on his shoulder. "Something you've never told anyone."

Jerel was silent for a moment, his gaze fixed on the fire. "I've done things I'm not proud of, Megan. Made choices that haunt me every day. But with you... I feel like I have a chance to be better."

Megan reached up, cupping his face in her hands. "We all have a past, Jerel. What matters is what we do with our future."

Jerel's eyes softened, filled with an emotion Megan couldn't quite place. "You make me wanna believe that, Megan. You make me wanna be a better man."

They kissed, the firelight casting flickering shadows across their faces. It was a kiss filled with promise, with the hope of a future free from the shadows of their pasts.

The days blurred together in a whirlwind of passion and connection. Megan and Jerel explored every inch of Cancun, from hidden waterfalls to bustling night markets. They danced under the stars, their bodies moving in perfect harmony, and shared intimate dinners that lasted long into the night.

Megan felt herself changing, growing stronger and more confident with each passing day. Jerel's presence was like a drug, intoxicating and addictive. She craved his touch, his words, the way he made her feel like the most important person in the world.

But as their time in paradise drew to a close, the reality of their separate worlds loomed over them like a dark cloud. Megan knew that their perfect bubble was about to burst, and the thought of returning to her old life without Jerel was unbearable.

On their last night in Cancun, Jerel arranged a private dinner on the beach. The setting was perfect – a table for two under a canopy of fairy lights, the sound of the waves providing a soothing backdrop. Megan wore a flowing dress, her hair loose and wild, feeling like a goddess under the moonlight.

Jerel took her hand, his eyes filled with an intensity that took her breath away. "Megan, this week has been everything I didn't know I needed. You've shown me a different side of life, one I want to hold on to."

Megan's heart pounded in her chest. "I feel the same, Jerel. But what happens now? We go back to our separate lives?"

Jerel shook his head, his grip tightening on her hand. "I don't want to lose you, Megan. We'll find a way to make this work. I promise you that."

They kissed, a kiss filled with desperation and longing. Megan felt tears prick her eyes, knowing that their time was running out. She wanted to believe in Jerel's promise, to hold on to the hope that they could find a way to be together.

Chapter 6: Unveiling Secrets

The air in Cancun was thick with the heat of the midday sun. Megan lay sprawled on a lounge chair by the pool, her thoughts drifting back to the intense, unforgettable moments she had shared with Jerel. She felt a warmth in her chest, a mixture of affection and desire. Her phone buzzed beside her, pulling her out of her reverie.

It was a message from Jerel: *Meet me at the marina at 4. I have a surprise for you.*

Megan's heart fluttered with excitement. She quickly gathered her things and headed back to her room to get ready. As she dressed, a part of her mind lingered on the things she didn't know about Jerel. She shook off the thoughts, deciding to focus on the present.

The marina was bustling with activity when Megan arrived. Boats of all shapes and sizes bobbed gently in the water, and the scent of salt and diesel filled the air. Jerel was waiting for her, leaning against a sleek, black speedboat. He looked up as she approached, a smile spreading across his face.

"Ready for an adventure?" he asked, holding out his hand to help her aboard.

Megan took his hand, feeling a jolt of electricity at his touch. "Always."

They sped across the water, the wind whipping through their hair and the roar of the engine drowning out all other sounds. Megan felt a rush of exhilaration, the thrill of the ride mixing with the excitement of being with Jerel. They reached a secluded cove and dropped anchor, the boat rocking gently in the calm waters.

Jerel handed her a snorkel mask and fins. "Ever been snorkeling?"

Megan shook her head, laughing. "No, but I'm game."

They dove into the crystal-clear water, exploring the vibrant underwater world together. Schools of colorful fish darted around them, and the coral reefs teemed with life. It was a magical experience, one that

Megan knew she would never forget. As they surfaced, Jerel pulled her close, his eyes dark with intensity.

"You're incredible, Megan," he murmured, his breath hot against her ear.

Megan felt a shiver run down her spine. "So are you, Jerel."

Later, as they lounged on the deck of the boat, Megan's curiosity got the better of her. "Jerel, can I ask you something?"

"Anything," he replied, his gaze steady.

She hesitated, then took a deep breath. "What exactly do you do for a living?"

Jerel's expression darkened slightly, but he didn't look away. "It's complicated, Megan. My life... it's not easy to explain."

Megan felt a pang of anxiety but pushed forward. "Try me."

Jerel sighed, running a hand through his hair. "I grew up in a tough neighborhood. Had to make some hard choices to survive. Now, I run things. Business is... dangerous. But it's what I know."

Megan's heart pounded in her chest. She had suspected that Jerel's life was far from ordinary, but hearing it confirmed was a shock. "Dangerous how?"

Jerel looked away, his jaw clenched. "Drugs, money, power. It's all part of the game. And it's a game that comes with a lot of risks."

Megan's mind raced. She knew she should be scared, should walk away from this man who lived a life so far removed from hers. But instead, she felt a strange sense of understanding and connection. "Jerel, I don't care about your past. I care about who you are now. And who you are to me."

Jerel turned back to her, his eyes filled with emotion. "You don't know what you're saying, Megan. My world could destroy you."

Megan reached out, cupping his face in her hands. "Then let's make a new world. Together."

That night, back at the resort, Megan lay awake, her mind a whirl of conflicting emotions. She knew the dangers that came with Jerel's lifestyle, but she also knew that her feelings for him were real and deep. She couldn't ignore the connection they shared, the way he made her feel alive and cherished.

As she tossed and turned, she heard a soft knock at her door. She opened it to find Jerel standing there, his expression troubled. "Can I come in?"

Megan stepped aside, allowing him to enter. "What's wrong?"

Jerel sat on the edge of the bed, his shoulders slumped. "I'm scared, Megan. Scared of what my life might do to you. But I can't walk away from you either."

Megan sat beside him, taking his hand in hers. "We'll figure it out, Jerel. One step at a time."

Jerel looked at her, his eyes filled with a mixture of hope and fear. "I've never met anyone like you, Megan. You make me want to be better."

Megan smiled, her heart swelling with love. "You already are, Jerel. You just need to believe it."

They kissed, a kiss filled with passion and promise. Megan knew that their journey together would be fraught with challenges, but she was ready to face them head-on. She couldn't imagine her life without Jerel, and she was determined to find a way to make it work.

Chapter 7: The Final Day

The morning sun peeked through the curtains of Megan's hotel room, casting a soft glow over the bed where she and Jerel lay entwined. The reality of their final day in Cancun loomed over them like a dark cloud. Megan sighed, running her fingers through Jerel's hair, wanting to hold onto this moment for as long as possible.

Jerel stirred, his eyes fluttering open. "Morning, beautiful."

Megan smiled, but it didn't reach her eyes. "Morning. I can't believe it's our last day here."

Jerel's expression turned serious. "I know. But this isn't the end for us, Megan. We'll find a way to make it work."

Megan nodded, trying to hold back the tears that threatened to spill. "I know. It's just... hard."

Jerel kissed her softly. "Let's make the most of today, okay?"

They spent the morning packing their bags, the silence heavy with unspoken emotions. Megan tried to focus on the task at hand, but her mind kept drifting back to the past week – the adventures, the laughter, the intense connection she had found with Jerel. She didn't want it to end.

Lila bounced into the room, her energy a stark contrast to Megan's somber mood. "Ready to head back to reality, Meg?"

Megan forced a smile. "As ready as I'll ever be."

Lila glanced at Jerel, raising an eyebrow. "Well, don't forget, what happens in Cancun stays in Cancun."

Megan's heart clenched at the thought. She didn't want Jerel to be just a memory. She wanted him to be a part of her life, no matter how complicated it might be.

They checked out of the hotel and headed to the airport, the journey filled with a bittersweet mix of nostalgia and dread. Megan held Jerel's hand tightly, afraid that letting go would mean losing him forever.

At the airport, they found a quiet corner to say their goodbyes. Jerel cupped Megan's face in his hands, his eyes filled with emotion. "This isn't goodbye, Megan. I promise you that."

Megan's voice trembled. "I believe you, Jerel. Just... be safe, okay?"

Jerel nodded, his jaw clenched. "You too, baby. I'll call you as soon as I land."

They kissed, a kiss filled with longing and desperation. Megan wanted to memorize every detail, every sensation, knowing it would have to sustain her until they could be together again.

The flight back home felt like an eternity. Megan stared out the window, her mind replaying the events of the past week. The excitement, the passion, the danger – it had all been so intense, so unlike anything she had ever experienced. She felt a deep ache in her chest, a void that Jerel had filled and now left empty.

Lila tried to cheer her up, but even her boundless energy couldn't lift Megan's spirits. "Come on, Meg, you'll see him again. You two are like... destiny or something."

Megan forced a smile. "I hope you're right."

Returning to her normal life felt like a harsh slap in the face. The bustling city, the endless noise, the suffocating routine – it all seemed so dull compared to the vibrant world she had shared with Jerel. Megan threw herself into her work, trying to drown out the emptiness with deadlines and meetings, but it was no use. Every spare moment, her thoughts drifted back to him.

One evening, as she sat in her apartment, her phone buzzed. It was a message from Jerel: *Miss you, baby. Can't wait to see you again.*

Megan's heart leapt. She quickly typed a response: *Miss you too. When can we meet?*

Jerel replied almost instantly: *Soon. Gotta handle some things first, but I'll be with you before you know it.*

Megan smiled, a small flicker of hope igniting in her chest. She could hold on to that, knowing that Jerel was out there, thinking of her too.

But as the days turned into weeks, the void Jerel had left behind grew deeper. Megan felt like a part of her was missing, a part she couldn't replace. She went through the motions of her daily life, but everything felt dull and colorless.

At night, she would lie in bed, her mind filled with memories of Cancun. The feel of Jerel's touch, the sound of his laugh, the intensity of his gaze – it all haunted her, a constant reminder of what she had lost. She clung to their nightly phone calls, each conversation a lifeline that kept her connected to him.

One evening, as she was getting ready for bed, her phone buzzed again. It was Jerel, but this time his message was different: *Need to talk. It's important.*

Megan's heart pounded as she called him. "What's wrong?"

Jerel's voice was tense. "Things are getting dangerous here, Megan. I need you to be careful. Don't tell anyone about us, okay? Not until I can sort this out."

Fear gripped Megan's heart. "What's happening, Jerel?"

"Just... trust me. I'll explain everything when I can. But for now, you need to stay safe."

Megan's mind raced, the implications of his words sinking in. "I trust you, Jerel. Just promise me you'll stay safe too."

"I promise, baby. I love you."

"I love you too."

Chapter 8: Separate Lives

Megan sat at her desk, her office bustling around her with the usual chaos of a Monday morning. She typed away at her computer, but her mind was elsewhere, drifting back to the sun-kissed beaches of Cancun and the intense connection she'd found with Jerel. The memory of his touch, his voice, his scent lingered in her thoughts, making it hard to focus on the stacks of legal briefs that awaited her attention.

"Earth to Megan," Lila called from the doorway, snapping Megan out of her reverie. "You've been zoning out a lot lately. Everything okay?"

Megan forced a smile. "Yeah, just a lot on my mind."

Lila raised an eyebrow. "Is this about Jerel? You've been different since you got back."

Megan sighed, rubbing her temples. "I can't stop thinking about him, Lila. It's like he's a part of me now, and I don't know how to let go."

Lila walked over and placed a comforting hand on Megan's shoulder. "Maybe you don't have to. Maybe you just need to find a way to make it work."

Megan nodded, appreciating the support but knowing that the reality of their separate lives was more complicated than that.

Meanwhile, Jerel was dealing with the gritty realities of his world. The dimly lit warehouse buzzed with activity, his crew hustling to pack and distribute the latest shipment. The smell of sweat and chemicals permeated the air, a stark contrast to the serene beaches he had shared with Megan.

Jerel stood in his office, staring at a map on the wall covered with red pins marking his territories. Dre, his right-hand man, entered the room, a look of concern on his face.

"JP, we got problems," Dre said, handing him a file. "Rival gangs are encroaching on our turf, and the cops are getting closer. We need to make some moves."

Jerel's jaw tightened as he flipped through the file. "We'll handle it. But we need to be smart. We can't afford any slip-ups."

Dre nodded, but his eyes lingered on Jerel. "You've been distracted lately, boss. Everything good?"

Jerel sighed, leaning back in his chair. "Just thinking about Megan. She's different, man. She makes me want to be better, but this life... it's hard to balance."

Dre shook his head, a hint of a smile playing on his lips. "Love'll do that to you. But you gotta stay focused. Can't let your guard down."

Jerel nodded, knowing Dre was right. He had to stay sharp, had to protect his empire, but the thought of Megan kept pulling at him, a reminder of the peace and happiness he'd found in her arms.

Days turned into weeks, and Megan threw herself into her work, trying to drown out the emptiness with deadlines and clients. She spent long hours at the office, her mind constantly drifting to Jerel, wondering what he was doing, if he was safe.

One night, as she was leaving the office, her phone buzzed with a message from Jerel: *Miss you, baby. Wish you were here.*

Megan's heart leapt, and she quickly typed a reply: *Miss you too. When can we see each other again?*

Jerel's response came swiftly: *Soon. Gotta handle some things first, but I promise, we'll be together again.*

Megan clung to those words, finding solace in their nightly phone calls. Each conversation was a lifeline, keeping their connection alive despite the distance and the dangers that surrounded Jerel's world.

Back in his world, Jerel was facing increasing pressure. Rival gangs were getting bolder, and the cops were closing in. The streets were a battleground, and every day was a struggle to maintain control. But through it all, Megan remained his anchor, the thought of her giving him strength and purpose.

One evening, after a particularly tense confrontation with a rival gang, Jerel found himself alone in his office, his thoughts drifting to

Megan. He pulled out his phone and called her, needing to hear her voice.

"Hey," Megan answered, her voice a soothing balm to his frayed nerves.

"Hey, baby. Just needed to hear you," Jerel said, leaning back in his chair.

Megan could hear the exhaustion in his voice. "Rough day?"

Jerel sighed. "Yeah. This life... it's a lot. But thinking about you makes it better."

Megan smiled, her heart aching with the distance between them. "I miss you, Jerel. I wish we could be together right now."

"Soon, Megan. I promise. I'm working on it."

Despite the challenges, Megan and Jerel's bond grew stronger. They found ways to support each other, to keep their connection alive. Megan's friends and colleagues noticed the change in her, the way her eyes lit up whenever she talked about Jerel, the way she seemed more alive, more vibrant.

But the reality of their separate lives was never far from her mind. Megan knew that their love was a fragile thing, constantly under threat from the dangers of Jerel's world. She worried about his safety, about the choices he had to make to survive.

Chapter 9: Maintaining Contact

The days blended into weeks, and Megan found herself clinging to her phone like a lifeline. Every evening, she would wait for Jerel's call, her heart racing with anticipation. Their conversations were a mix of sweet nothings and gritty reality checks, each word strengthening their bond despite the miles between them.

Megan sat in her apartment, the city lights casting a soft glow through the window. Her phone buzzed, and she quickly answered, her heart skipping a beat. "Hey, you," she said, her voice soft and warm.

"Hey, baby," Jerel's deep voice rumbled through the line. "How's your day been?"

Megan sighed, leaning back on the couch. "Busy as hell. Work never seems to let up. But hearing your voice makes it all better."

Jerel chuckled, the sound sending shivers down her spine. "You keep saying sweet things like that, and I might just hop on a plane to see you."

Megan laughed, the tension of the day melting away. "Don't tempt me. How are things on your end?"

Jerel's tone grew serious. "You know how it is. Business as usual, dealing with the usual bullshit. But I'm managing. Thinking about you keeps me sane."

Despite the chaos of their lives, Megan and Jerel found solace in their nightly conversations. They talked about everything – their dreams, their fears, their plans for the future. Jerel shared stories from his past, tales of survival and street smarts, while Megan opened up about her struggles and aspirations. Each story, each shared secret, drew them closer together.

One night, Jerel's voice was filled with a rare vulnerability. "You ever think about what it would be like if we were just... normal? No bullshit, no danger. Just you and me, living a simple life."

Megan's heart ached at the thought. "All the time, Jerel. But I believe we can find our own version of normal. We just have to keep fighting for it."

Jerel was silent for a moment, then he spoke, his voice tinged with determination. "I'm working on it, Megan. For us."

Meanwhile, their lives continued on separate tracks, each dealing with their own struggles and battles. Megan threw herself into her work, her mind constantly drifting back to Jerel. She found herself looking forward to their calls, the highlight of her day. Her colleagues noticed the change in her – the way her eyes sparkled when she talked about him, the way she seemed more alive.

"Megan, you've got it bad," Lila teased one afternoon as they grabbed lunch. "I've never seen you like this."

Megan smiled, a dreamy look in her eyes. "I can't help it, Lila. He's everything I never knew I needed."

Lila's expression turned serious. "Just be careful, Meg. His world... it's dangerous."

Megan nodded, her smile fading. "I know. But I trust him. And I believe in us."

Jerel was grappling with the harsh realities of his world. The pressure was mounting – rival gangs were pushing into his territory, and the cops were tightening their grip. But through it all, thoughts of Megan kept him going, gave him a reason to push through the darkness.

Dre noticed the change in his boss. "JP, you seem different. Calmer. What's going on?"

Jerel smirked, leaning back in his chair. "It's Megan. She gives me something to fight for. Makes me want to be better."

Dre shook his head, a smile playing on his lips. "Love does that, man. Just don't let it get you killed."

Jerel's expression turned serious. "I won't. But I'm not giving her up, either."

As the weeks passed, Megan and Jerel's bond grew stronger, their connection deepening despite the distance. They found ways to stay close, to keep their love alive. Megan sent Jerel photos and videos of her day-to-day life, while Jerel shared glimpses of his world – the good, the bad, and the ugly.

One evening, Jerel called, his voice filled with a mix of excitement and anxiety. "Megan, I need to see you. I can't keep doing this over the phone."

Megan's heart raced. "When? Where?"

"I'll come to you. Just give me some time to sort things out here."

Megan's pulse quickened with anticipation. "I'll be waiting, Jerel. Just be safe, okay?"

"I will, baby. I promise."

Their calls became more frequent, more intimate. Megan felt herself falling deeper for Jerel, her feelings for him intensifying with each passing day. She knew that their love was fraught with danger, but she couldn't imagine her life without him.

One night, as Megan lay in bed, her phone buzzed with a message from Jerel: *I'm coming to see you soon. Can't wait to hold you again.*

Megan's heart soared as she typed a reply: *I can't wait either. Hurry back to me.*

The anticipation of their reunion kept her going, gave her something to look forward to. She knew that their lives were complicated, filled with danger and uncertainty, but she believed in their love. She believed that they could find a way to be together, no matter what obstacles lay in their path.

Chapter 10: Secrets and Danger

The sound of sirens echoed through the dark streets, blending with the low hum of city life. Jerel stood in the shadows, his eyes scanning the alleyway as Dre spoke in hushed tones with a group of men. Tension hung heavy in the air, each moment thick with the threat of violence.

"Boss, we got a problem," Dre muttered, turning to Jerel with a grim expression. "The cops are tightening their grip. They're onto us, and we got rival crews sniffing around our turf."

Jerel's jaw clenched, the weight of his empire pressing down on him. "We need to move smart, Dre. No mistakes. Keep the heat off us and handle those rivals. I don't care how."

Dre nodded, but his eyes held a flicker of doubt. "You sure you can handle all this, JP? You've been distracted lately."

Jerel's gaze hardened. "I can handle it. Just do your job."

Megan sat in her apartment, her mind racing. She had spent the evening researching, trying to uncover more about Jerel's world. The more she discovered, the deeper her concern grew. News articles, police reports, and whispered rumors painted a dark picture of the man she had fallen for.

Her phone buzzed with a message from Jerel: *Miss you, baby. Can't wait to see you.*

Megan's heart ached as she typed a reply: *Miss you too. Be safe.*

She needed to talk to someone, to get a handle on the turmoil inside her. Lila's words of warning echoed in her mind, but she couldn't bring herself to walk away from Jerel. Not yet.

Jerel returned to his apartment, the weight of the night's events heavy on his shoulders. He collapsed onto the couch, his mind swirling with thoughts of Megan. She was the one bright spot in his dark world, the one thing that kept him going.

As he closed his eyes, the memories of his past began to surface. The choices he had made, the lives he had destroyed – it all haunted him, but he couldn't escape it. He was too deep in the game to turn back now.

Megan decided to confront Jerel, needing to understand the full extent of his life. She dialed his number, her heart pounding as she waited for him to answer.

"Hey, baby," Jerel's voice was a soothing balm to her frayed nerves.

"Jerel, we need to talk," Megan said, her voice trembling. "I've been doing some research... about you."

There was a long silence on the other end of the line. "What did you find?"

"Everything. The drugs, the violence, the cops... Jerel, why didn't you tell me?"

Jerel sighed heavily. "I wanted to protect you, Megan. My world is dangerous, and I didn't want you to get hurt."

Megan's anger flared. "But I'm already involved, Jerel. I love you, and I can't just ignore what you do."

"I know," Jerel said, his voice pained. "But I'm trying to change. For you. For us."

Megan's heart softened, but the fear still gnawed at her. "You have to promise me, Jerel. No more secrets. If we're going to make this work, I need to know everything."

"I promise, Megan. No more secrets," Jerel said, his voice filled with determination. "Just trust me."

The days that followed were filled with tension and uncertainty. Jerel's world was closing in on him, the dangers mounting with each passing hour. He moved cautiously, aware that any misstep could bring everything crashing down.

One night, as he was meeting with his crew, a group of armed men stormed the warehouse. Shots rang out, the air filled with the acrid smell of gunpowder and the sounds of chaos.

Jerel ducked behind a stack of crates, his mind racing. "Dre, get everyone out! Now!"

Dre nodded, barking orders to the crew as they fought their way to safety. Jerel's thoughts flickered to Megan, the fear for her safety driving him to fight harder. He couldn't let anything happen to her.

Megan paced her apartment, the anxiety gnawing at her insides. She hadn't heard from Jerel in hours, and the fear that something had happened to him was overwhelming. Her phone buzzed with a call, and she quickly answered, her heart in her throat.

"Jerel?"

"Megan, I'm okay," Jerel's voice was strained, but alive. "We had some trouble, but we're safe now."

Megan's relief was palpable. "Thank God. I was so worried."

"I know, baby. I'm sorry. But I need you to be strong. Things are getting more dangerous, and I need to know you're safe."

Megan's resolve hardened. "I am strong, Jerel. And I'm not going anywhere."

Jerel's world grew darker, the threats more intense. The rival gangs were relentless, and the police were closing in. Each day was a battle for survival, but through it all, Megan remained his anchor, the one thing that kept him grounded.

One evening, as he sat in his apartment, Jerel made a decision. He picked up his phone and called Megan.

"Hey, baby," Megan answered, her voice a balm to his weary soul.

"Megan, I need to see you. I can't keep doing this over the phone."

"When?"

"Tomorrow. I'll be there."

Chapter 11: Reunion

Jerel paced his apartment, the weight of his decisions pressing down on him. He had arranged for Megan to visit, despite knowing the risks. The anticipation gnawed at him, and he couldn't shake the feeling that this reunion would be a turning point for them both.

"Dre, everything set?" Jerel asked, his voice tense.

Dre nodded, his face serious. "Yeah, boss. Got extra eyes on the place. We'll make sure nothing happens."

Jerel exhaled, his mind already racing through the possible scenarios. "Good. I need this to go smoothly. She means everything to me, man."

Dre clapped a hand on Jerel's shoulder. "I get it. We'll keep her safe."

Megan's heart pounded as she stepped off the plane, her nerves a tangled mess of excitement and fear. She clutched her bag tightly, scanning the crowd for Jerel. When she finally spotted him, her breath caught in her throat. He looked the same but different – the same intense eyes, the same commanding presence, but with a new edge of weariness.

"Jerel," she breathed, rushing into his arms.

He pulled her close, burying his face in her hair. "God, I missed you, Megan."

They stood like that for a long moment, the world around them fading away. Megan felt tears sting her eyes, the reality of their reunion sinking in. She pulled back slightly, looking up at him.

"I missed you too," she whispered.

Jerel cupped her face in his hands, his eyes searching hers. "You're here now. That's all that matters."

The drive to Jerel's place was tense, the streets teeming with life and danger. Megan stared out the window, taking in the gritty reality of his world. She felt a mixture of fear and determination – fear for the dangers that surrounded them, and determination to be with Jerel no matter what.

When they finally arrived, Jerel led her inside, his grip on her hand firm. The apartment was a mix of luxury and security, the contrast stark and unsettling.

"Welcome to my world," Jerel said, his voice tinged with irony.

Megan looked around, taking in the high-end furniture, the state-of-the-art security systems, and the faint smell of gun oil that lingered in the air. "It's... different."

Jerel laughed softly. "Yeah, you could say that."

They settled onto the couch, the tension between them thick with unspoken words. Jerel leaned back, his eyes dark with emotion.

"Megan, I know this isn't easy. But I need you to understand... this is my life. It's messy and dangerous, but it's all I know."

Megan reached for his hand, her fingers intertwining with his. "I get that, Jerel. And I'm not asking you to change overnight. I just want to be with you, to support you."

Jerel's gaze softened, a rare vulnerability shining through. "I don't deserve you, Megan. But I'm damn sure not letting you go."

Their reunion was a whirlwind of emotions – passion, fear, hope, and doubt all crashing together in a storm of intensity. Megan felt like she was drowning in Jerel's presence, overwhelmed by the depth of her feelings for him.

That night, they lay entwined in bed, the city's noise a distant hum outside the window. Megan traced the lines of Jerel's tattoos, each one telling a story of his life and the battles he had fought.

"Tell me about this one," she said, her fingers lingering on a dragon wrapped around his bicep.

Jerel looked down at her, a faint smile on his lips. "Got that after my first big deal. Thought I was invincible. Turns out, I was just stupid."

Megan kissed the tattoo, feeling the weight of his words. "You're not stupid, Jerel. You're strong. And you've survived things most people couldn't imagine."

Jerel sighed, his eyes closing. "You give me too much credit, Megan. But I'll take it, if it means I get to keep you."

Megan snuggled closer, her heart full. "You're stuck with me now."

The next few days were a mix of normalcy and chaos. Jerel took Megan around the city, showing her the parts of his life he could share. They visited his favorite spots, shared meals with his crew, and even found moments of peace amidst the madness.

But the danger was never far away. Jerel's phone buzzed constantly with updates from Dre, the tension in his shoulders never fully easing. Megan saw the strain, the way he carried the weight of his world on his back, and it made her heart ache.

One evening, as they sat on the balcony overlooking the city, Jerel's phone buzzed again. He glanced at it, his expression darkening.

"Trouble?" Megan asked, her voice soft.

Jerel nodded, his jaw tight. "Always."

Megan took his hand, squeezing it gently. "We'll get through this, Jerel. Together."

Jerel looked at her, his eyes filled with a mix of love and fear. "I hope you're right, Megan. Because I don't know what I'd do without you."

Chapter 12: Into the Fire

Megan woke up to the distant sound of gunshots, her heart pounding in her chest. She sat up in bed, the room still dark, and reached for Jerel, who was already awake, his eyes fixed on the window.

"Stay here," he whispered, his voice tense.

Megan's mind raced, fear gripping her. "Jerel, what's happening?"

"Nothing good," Jerel replied, grabbing his gun from the nightstand. "I need to check on things. Promise me you'll stay here."

Megan nodded, her throat tight. "Be careful."

Jerel kissed her forehead, his touch lingering. "Always."

He slipped out of the room, and Megan's anxiety grew with every passing second. The sounds of the night, usually a comforting background hum, now felt threatening and close. She hated feeling helpless, but she knew Jerel needed her to stay safe.

Minutes felt like hours before Jerel returned, his face grim. "We got trouble. Rival crew tried to hit one of our spots."

Megan's heart sank. "Is everyone okay?"

Jerel nodded, his eyes hard. "For now. But it's getting worse. They're pushing hard, trying to take us down."

Megan reached for him, her hands trembling. "What can I do?"

Jerel sat beside her, his shoulders heavy with the weight of his world. "Just stay close. We'll get through this."

The next few days were a blur of tension and close calls. Megan got a firsthand look at the dangers of Jerel's life, and it was a harsh, unforgiving reality. She saw the way he commanded his crew, the way he navigated the constant threats with a mix of cunning and force.

One afternoon, they were driving through the city when a car suddenly swerved into their path, forcing them to a screeching halt. Jerel's eyes flashed with anger as he reached for his gun.

"Stay down!" he barked, pushing Megan's head below the dashboard.

Bullets shattered the car windows, and Megan's heart raced in her chest. She clung to the seat, her mind filled with images of Jerel getting hurt, or worse. The sound of gunfire was deafening, and she prayed for it to end.

Jerel returned fire, his movements precise and controlled. Megan stole a glance at him, seeing the fierce determination in his eyes. He was fighting not just for his life, but for hers too.

After what felt like an eternity, the gunfire ceased, and Jerel checked the surroundings. "We're clear. Let's go."

They sped away, Megan's hands shaking as she clutched the seat. Jerel's jaw was clenched, his eyes scanning the streets for any sign of further danger.

"Are you okay?" he asked, his voice softer now.

Megan nodded, tears welling up in her eyes. "Yeah, I'm okay. But that was... intense."

Jerel reached over, squeezing her hand. "I'm sorry you had to see that. But this is my life, Megan. And it's not going to change overnight."

Megan took a deep breath, her fear mingling with a fierce resolve. "I know. And I'm not going anywhere. We'll get through this together."

Despite the dangers, Megan and Jerel's bond grew stronger. They found solace in each other, their love deepening with every shared moment. Megan saw the man behind the kingpin – the man who cared deeply, who wanted a better life for them both.

One evening, they sat on the rooftop, the city lights twinkling below them. Jerel pulled Megan close, his eyes filled with a rare vulnerability.

"You know, you're the best thing that's ever happened to me," he said, his voice low.

Megan smiled, her heart swelling with love. "You're pretty amazing yourself, Jerel."

Jerel's gaze turned serious. "I'm going to make this work, Megan. I'm going to get us out of this mess. I promise you that."

Megan kissed him, their connection electric. "I believe you. And I'm with you, no matter what."

The nights were filled with whispered promises and stolen moments of peace. Jerel's touch was both fierce and tender, his presence a constant reminder of the life they were fighting for. Megan felt herself falling deeper, her love for him consuming her in ways she had never imagined.

But the dangers were never far away. Each day brought new challenges, new threats. Jerel's rivals were relentless, and the law enforcement pressure was intensifying. Megan saw the toll it was taking on him, the way it wore him down.

One night, as they lay in bed, Jerel's phone buzzed with an urgent message. He read it, his expression darkening.

"I have to go," he said, his voice grim.

Megan's heart sank. "Be careful."

Jerel kissed her, his eyes filled with a mixture of love and determination. "Always."

Chapter 13: Increasing Stakes

The streets were ablaze with tension, the atmosphere thick with an underlying menace that seemed to touch every corner of Jerel's empire. Jerel stood in his office, staring out at the city that he had fought so hard to control. His phone buzzed constantly, delivering a steady stream of bad news. Rival crews were getting bolder, and law enforcement was closing in.

"Dre, what's the latest?" Jerel asked, turning to his right-hand man.

Dre's face was grim. "We got intel that the G-Mob is planning a major move on our territory. They're gunning for us, hard."

Jerel's eyes narrowed, his mind racing. "We need to hit them before they hit us. Mobilize the crew. And Dre, no mistakes. We can't afford any slip-ups now."

Dre nodded, but there was a flicker of concern in his eyes. "You sure about this, JP? Things are getting real heated out there."

Jerel's expression hardened. "I don't have a choice. It's us or them."

Meanwhile, Megan sat in the apartment, staring at the ceiling. Her mind was a whirlwind of thoughts and emotions. She loved Jerel with a fierceness that scared her, but the reality of his world was starting to take its toll. The constant danger, the violence, the uncertainty – it was all becoming too much to bear.

Lila's voice echoed in her mind, a reminder of the warnings she had tried to ignore. "Just be careful, Meg. His world... it's dangerous."

Megan sighed, rubbing her temples. She had seen firsthand the risks Jerel faced every day, and the thought of losing him was unbearable. But staying with him meant living a life on the edge, always looking over her shoulder.

Her phone buzzed, and she glanced at the screen. It was a message from Jerel: *Need to see you. Meet me at the spot.

Megan's heart skipped a beat. She quickly grabbed her things and headed out, the familiar mix of excitement and dread bubbling up inside her.

The spot was a small, hidden café where Jerel and Megan could meet away from prying eyes. When Megan arrived, Jerel was already there, his face drawn with tension. He looked up as she approached, his eyes softening at the sight of her.

"Hey, baby," he said, pulling her into a tight embrace.

Megan held him close, savoring the moment of peace. "Hey. What's going on?"

Jerel led her to a secluded booth, his expression serious. "Things are getting real bad, Megan. Rival crews are pushing hard, and the cops are on our backs. I'm trying to keep us safe, but it's getting harder every day."

Megan's heart ached for him. "What can I do to help?"

Jerel shook his head, his eyes filled with a mixture of love and frustration. "Just be here. Be with me. That's all I need."

Megan reached across the table, taking his hand in hers. "I'm not going anywhere, Jerel. But I need you to promise me something."

"Anything," he said, his voice soft.

"Promise me you'll stay safe. I can't lose you."

Jerel's grip tightened on her hand. "I promise, Megan. I'll do everything I can to keep us both safe."

The power struggles intensified, and Jerel's world grew darker by the day. He was constantly on the move, coordinating attacks, defending his turf, and trying to outmaneuver both his rivals and the police. The stress was taking its toll, and Megan could see it in his eyes, the way he carried himself.

One night, as they lay in bed, Megan turned to him, her voice trembling. "Jerel, how long can we keep doing this?"

Jerel stared at the ceiling, his jaw clenched. "I don't know, Megan. But I'm fighting for us. For our future."

Megan's eyes filled with tears. "I'm scared, Jerel. Scared of losing you, of getting caught up in something I can't handle."

Jerel pulled her close, his touch gentle yet firm. "I'm scared too, baby. But I can't walk away. Not now. Not when we're so close."

Megan buried her face in his chest, her heart heavy with fear and love. "Just promise me you'll be careful."

"I promise," Jerel whispered, his voice filled with determination.

As the days went on, the stakes continued to rise. Jerel found himself in increasingly dangerous situations, his life and his empire hanging by a thread. The rival crews were relentless, and the police were closing in, their net tightening around him.

Megan watched from the sidelines, her heart in her throat every time Jerel walked out the door. She wanted to be strong, to support him, but the constant fear was wearing her down.

One evening, Jerel returned home with a fresh cut on his forehead, blood trickling down his face. Megan's breath caught in her throat as she rushed to him.

"What happened?" she cried, her hands trembling as she reached for a cloth to clean the wound.

Jerel winced but managed a reassuring smile. "Just a close call. Nothing I couldn't handle."

Megan's eyes filled with tears. "This isn't sustainable, Jerel. You can't keep living like this."

Jerel's expression turned serious. "I know, Megan. And I'm working on a way out. But until then, we have to stay strong. We have to fight."

Chapter 14: Breaking Point

The night was tense, the air heavy with the threat of impending violence. Jerel's enemies were closing in, and everyone in his crew could feel the pressure. The city streets buzzed with an uneasy energy, a sense of foreboding that seemed to seep into every corner.

Jerel stood in his office, staring at a map marked with the territories in dispute. Dre stood beside him, his face grim.

"JP, we got intel that the G-Mob is planning a full-scale attack tonight. They want to take us out, once and for all."

Jerel's jaw tightened. "We can't let that happen. Get everyone ready. We're gonna meet them head-on."

Dre nodded, his eyes hard. "You got it, boss."

Jerel turned to his phone, his thoughts drifting to Megan. He didn't want her anywhere near this chaos, but he knew she would worry if he didn't check in.

"Hey, baby," he said when she answered. "Things are heating up. I need you to stay inside tonight, okay? Don't open the door for anyone."

Megan's voice was filled with concern. "What's going on, Jerel? Are you in danger?"

"Nothing I can't handle," Jerel replied, trying to sound reassuring. "Just promise me you'll stay safe."

"I promise," Megan said, her voice trembling. "Just come back to me in one piece."

The hours passed in a blur of preparation and tension. Jerel's crew was on high alert, their weapons ready, their eyes scanning the streets for any sign of movement. The calm before the storm was almost unbearable.

Suddenly, the sound of gunfire shattered the night. Jerel's heart pounded as he rushed outside, his men already engaged in a fierce battle with the rival gang. Bullets flew, the air thick with smoke and chaos.

Jerel moved with precision, his focus sharp. He had been in countless battles before, but this one felt different. The stakes were higher, the danger more imminent. He couldn't afford to lose tonight – not with so much on the line.

Dre was at his side, firing with deadly accuracy. "We gotta push them back, JP. They're coming at us hard."

Jerel nodded, his jaw set. "Let's do it."

The battle raged on, the sounds of violence echoing through the streets. Jerel's mind was a whirlwind of strategy and survival, but through it all, one thought kept him grounded: Megan. He had to make it through this for her.

Megan paced the apartment, her anxiety growing with each passing minute. She could hear the distant sounds of gunfire, and her heart ached with fear for Jerel. She hated feeling so helpless, trapped in a world she didn't fully understand.

Her phone buzzed, and she quickly answered, her voice shaky. "Jerel?"

"Megan, it's Dre," came the reply. "Jerel's handling business. He told me to check on you."

Megan's heart skipped a beat. "Is he okay?"

"He's holding his own," Dre said, his voice steady. "But it's bad out here. Real bad."

Megan took a deep breath, trying to calm her racing heart. "I need to see him, Dre. I need to know he's okay."

"Stay where you are," Dre insisted. "It's too dangerous."

Megan's resolve hardened. "I'm coming. I can't just sit here and do nothing."

Before Dre could argue, Megan hung up and grabbed the extra keys. Her mind was made up – she had to be with Jerel, no matter the risk.

The streets were chaotic, filled with the sounds of sirens and gunfire. Megan drove with determination, her fear giving way to a fierce need to be by Jerel's side. She knew she was venturing into dangerous territory, but she couldn't turn back now.

When she arrived at the scene, she was met with a wall of chaos. Jerel's men were fighting desperately, holding their ground against the rival crew. Megan's eyes searched the crowd frantically, her heart racing.

Then she saw him. Jerel was in the thick of the battle, his face set with grim determination. He moved with a lethal grace, his every action precise and controlled. Megan's heart ached with a mixture of fear and admiration.

"Jerel!" she called out, her voice barely audible over the noise.

Jerel's head snapped up, his eyes widening in shock when he saw her. "Megan, what the hell are you doing here?"

"I couldn't stay away," she said, her voice breaking. "I had to see you."

Jerel's expression softened, but there was no time for tenderness. "Get down! It's too dangerous!"

Megan ducked behind a car, her heart pounding. She watched as Jerel fought, her fear mingling with a fierce pride. He was risking everything for his crew, for his territory, for her.

The battle felt like it lasted forever, but finally, the gunfire ceased. Jerel's crew had managed to push back the rival gang, but the cost had been high. Bodies lay strewn across the ground, and the air was thick with the smell of smoke and blood.

Jerel rushed to Megan, his face etched with worry. "Are you okay?"

Megan nodded, tears streaming down her face. "I'm fine. But you..."

Jerel pulled her into a tight embrace, his body trembling with the aftermath of the battle. "I'm okay, baby. I'm okay."

Megan clung to him, her heart heavy with the weight of what they had just been through. She knew this was a turning point, a moment of reckoning.

"Jerel, I can't keep living like this," she said, her voice barely a whisper. "I love you, but this life... it's tearing me apart."

Jerel's grip tightened on her. "I know, Megan. I know. But I need you. I need us to be strong. Just a little longer."

Megan looked into his eyes, seeing the desperation and love there. She knew she had a choice to make – stay with him and face the dangers, or walk away and protect her own heart.

"I'll stay," she said, her voice firm. "But you have to promise me something."

"Anything," Jerel said, his eyes intense.

"Promise me we'll find a way out. Together."

Jerel nodded, his voice filled with determination. "I promise, Megan. We'll find a way."

Chapter 15: Love and Loyalty

The aftermath of the battle left the streets littered with debris and echoes of gunfire. Jerel's crew was battered but standing, their eyes reflecting the resolve they shared. Among them, Megan stood out, her presence a testament to her unwavering love for Jerel.

As the sun began to rise, casting a pale light over the city, Jerel pulled Megan into a tight embrace. "You shouldn't have come," he whispered, his voice a mix of relief and concern.

Megan looked up at him, her eyes fierce. "I had to. I can't sit back and watch from the sidelines, Jerel. I'm in this with you."

Jerel's heart swelled with emotion. He kissed her forehead, his grip on her tightening. "We'll get through this. Together."

The days that followed were a blur of strategy meetings and security upgrades. Jerel's apartment became a fortress, every entry point monitored, every window reinforced. His crew was on high alert, their eyes constantly scanning for threats.

Megan adapted quickly, her resolve unshaken. She found herself learning the intricacies of Jerel's world, understanding the unspoken rules and the silent signals that governed their lives. She was no longer an outsider looking in; she was part of the family now.

One evening, as the city lights flickered in the distance, Megan and Jerel sat on the balcony, the weight of their decisions pressing down on them.

"Are you sure about this?" Jerel asked, his voice low.

Megan nodded, her eyes never leaving his. "I've never been more sure of anything. I love you, Jerel. And I'm not going anywhere."

Jerel's eyes softened, a rare vulnerability shining through. "I don't deserve you, Megan. But I'm grateful every day that you're here."

Megan leaned in, her lips brushing against his. "We deserve each other. And we'll fight for our future, no matter what."

Their resolve was tested daily. Rival crews were relentless, each encounter a reminder of the dangers that surrounded them. Megan stood by Jerel through it all, her love and loyalty a constant source of strength.

One night, as they were driving through a particularly rough part of town, their car was ambushed. Gunfire erupted, and Jerel's instincts kicked in. He swerved, maneuvering through the chaos with a precision that left Megan in awe.

"Get down!" Jerel shouted, his voice cutting through the noise.

Megan obeyed, her heart racing as bullets shattered the windows. She clung to the seat, her mind racing with fear and determination. She knew that every day with Jerel meant facing these dangers, but she was willing to do whatever it took to stay by his side.

Jerel returned fire, his movements calculated and lethal. Within minutes, the ambush was over, the rival crew retreating into the shadows. Jerel reached over, his hand finding Megan's. "You okay?"

Megan nodded, her breath coming in shaky bursts. "Yeah, I'm okay. Just... scared."

Jerel squeezed her hand, his eyes filled with a mix of love and regret. "I'm sorry, Megan. This is my world. But I promise you, we'll find a way out."

Megan's heart ached for him. "I know, Jerel. And I'll be with you every step of the way."

Despite the constant threats, Megan and Jerel's bond grew stronger. They faced each challenge head-on, their love solidifying with each shared victory and every narrow escape. Jerel's crew began to see Megan not just as Jerel's woman, but as a vital part of their family.

One evening, Dre approached Megan, his expression thoughtful. "You're tougher than I gave you credit for," he admitted. "Jerel's lucky to have you."

Megan smiled, her eyes filled with determination. "We're lucky to have each other. And we're going to make it through this."

Dre nodded, a hint of respect in his eyes. "I believe you. And we've got your back."

As the weeks passed, Megan and Jerel continued to navigate the dangers of their world. They found solace in each other, their love a beacon of hope in the darkness that surrounded them. Each day was a battle, but together, they were unstoppable.

One night, as they lay in bed, Jerel's arms wrapped around Megan, he whispered, "We're getting closer to finding a way out. Just a little longer."

Megan snuggled closer, her heart filled with love and determination. "I believe in us, Jerel. We'll make it."

But the city had a way of reminding them that peace was always just out of reach. One evening, as they walked hand in hand through a quiet neighborhood, a shadowy figure stepped into their path. Jerel's body tensed, his eyes narrowing.

"Jerel Phillips," the figure said, his voice dripping with menace. "We've got unfinished business."

Jerel pushed Megan behind him, his hand moving to his concealed weapon. "Stay out of this, Megan."

Megan's heart pounded, but she stood her ground. "I'm not leaving you."

The figure laughed, a cold, chilling sound. "How touching. But this ends tonight."

The tension was palpable, the air thick with the threat of violence. Megan's mind raced, her love for Jerel fueling her determination. She knew that this was another test, another challenge they had to face together.

Jerel's eyes never left the figure. "If you want a fight, you've got one. But you'll have to get through me first."

Chapter 16: The Ultimate Test

The night air was thick with tension, the streets of the city echoing with an uneasy calm. Jerel had felt the shift in the atmosphere, the subtle undercurrent of betrayal that gnawed at his instincts. He sat in his office, the dim light casting shadows across his face as he reviewed the plans for their next move. Dre entered, his expression serious.

"JP, we got intel on a possible hit. Word is, someone close might be playing both sides," Dre said, his voice low.

Jerel's eyes narrowed. "Who?"

Dre hesitated, a flicker of doubt crossing his face. "T, man. He's been acting real shady lately."

Jerel's jaw clenched. T had been a trusted ally for years, someone who had earned his place in the crew through loyalty and grit. The idea of betrayal stung deep, but Jerel knew better than to ignore Dre's gut feeling.

"Keep an eye on him. And be ready for anything," Jerel ordered, his mind already racing with contingency plans.

Megan was in the kitchen, preparing a late dinner when Jerel walked in. His presence was a mix of tension and determination, and she could see the storm brewing behind his eyes.

"What's wrong?" she asked, her voice filled with concern.

Jerel pulled her into a tight embrace, his hands gripping her shoulders. "We might have a traitor in our midst. I need you to be extra careful, Megan. Don't trust anyone."

Megan's heart sank. "Do you know who it is?"

Jerel nodded. "I have my suspicions. But until I know for sure, I need to protect you. Promise me you'll stay safe."

Megan looked into his eyes, her resolve firm. "I promise. But I'm not leaving your side."

Jerel's eyes softened. "I wouldn't have it any other way."

Later that night, the tension came to a head. Jerel and his crew gathered in the warehouse, a sense of impending danger hanging over them. T was there, his eyes shifting nervously as he tried to blend in. Jerel watched him closely, his instincts screaming that something was about to go down.

As they reviewed the plan, T suddenly stepped back, pulling a gun from his waistband. "I'm sorry, JP. They made me do it."

Chaos erupted. Shots were fired, and the air filled with the sound of gunfire and shouts. Jerel dove behind a stack of crates, his mind racing. He needed to protect his crew, protect Megan, and survive this betrayal.

"Dre, cover me!" Jerel shouted, his voice barely audible over the cacophony.

Dre nodded, his gun blazing as he provided cover fire. Jerel moved with lethal precision, taking out enemies with cold efficiency. He spotted T trying to escape, and anger surged through him.

"T, you motherfucker!" Jerel roared, his voice filled with rage.

T turned, fear in his eyes. "JP, I had no choice! They threatened my family!"

Jerel's grip on his gun tightened. "You betrayed me. There's no coming back from that."

Before T could respond, Jerel fired, the bullet hitting its mark. T fell to the ground, the betrayal etched on his face as he took his last breath.

Megan had taken cover in a back room, her heart pounding with fear. She clutched a small handgun, the weight of it unfamiliar and terrifying. She could hear the chaos outside, the sounds of battle and betrayal.

Suddenly, the door burst open, and an enemy rushed in. Megan's instincts kicked in, and she fired, the shot hitting the intruder in the chest. He fell to the ground, and Megan's hands shook with adrenaline.

Jerel burst in moments later, his eyes wide with concern. "Megan, you okay?"

Megan nodded, tears streaming down her face. "I think so. I... I shot him, Jerel."

Jerel pulled her into his arms, his voice soothing. "You did what you had to. You saved yourself. I'm so proud of you."

Megan clung to him, her fear mingling with relief. "What now?"

"We finish this," Jerel said, his voice filled with determination.

The battle raged on, Jerel and his crew fighting for their lives. They moved as one, their loyalty to each other unbreakable. Megan stayed close to Jerel, her fear giving way to a fierce resolve. She was part of this world now, and she would fight for it with everything she had.

The gunfire finally ceased. Jerel stood amidst the wreckage, his chest heaving with exhaustion. The rival crew had been defeated, but the cost had been high.

Dre approached, his face bruised but determined. "We did it, JP. We took them down."

Jerel nodded, his eyes scanning the battlefield. "We did. But we lost good men today."

Megan stepped forward, her hand finding Jerel's. "And we survived. Together."

Jerel looked at her, his eyes filled with a mix of love and gratitude. "Yeah, we did. And we'll keep fighting. For us."

Chapter 17: Climactic Showdown

The tension in the air was palpable as Jerel and his crew prepared for the final confrontation. They gathered in the warehouse, the dim lighting casting long shadows over their determined faces. Jerel stood at the center, his eyes scanning his men. He knew this battle would change everything.

"Listen up," Jerel began, his voice low but commanding. "This is it. The G-Mob wants to take us out, and we ain't gonna let that happen. We fight for our turf, for our families, for each other. We go in strong, and we come out on top. No room for fear. No room for mistakes."

Dre stepped forward, his expression fierce. "We got your back, JP. All the way."

Jerel nodded, his resolve solidified by the loyalty of his crew. He turned to Megan, who stood by his side, her eyes filled with determination and fear. "You ready for this?"

Megan took a deep breath, her heart pounding. "I'm ready. Let's end this."

The streets were eerily quiet as they made their way to the rendezvous point. Jerel's crew moved with the stealth and precision of seasoned fighters, each one prepared for the bloody battle that awaited them. Megan stayed close to Jerel, her heart a mix of fear and fierce resolve.

As they approached the abandoned factory where the G-Mob had set up, Jerel raised his hand, signaling for silence. The air was thick with tension, every shadow a potential threat. They crept forward, their weapons at the ready.

Suddenly, a shout rang out, and the night exploded with gunfire. Bullets whizzed past them, the air filled with the deafening sounds of battle. Jerel ducked behind a stack of crates, returning fire with lethal precision.

"Dre, take the left flank! Cover fire!" Jerel barked, his voice cutting through the chaos.

Dre nodded, leading a group of men around the side of the building. Megan crouched beside Jerel, her hands trembling as she aimed her gun at the shadows.

"Stay close to me," Jerel said, his voice fierce. "We get through this together."

Megan nodded, her eyes locked on the scene before her. The factory was a warzone, filled with smoke and the sounds of struggle. She watched as Jerel moved with deadly grace, his every action a testament to his skill and determination.

The battle raged on, each side fighting with desperate intensity. Jerel's crew pushed forward, their loyalty and strength driving them through the chaos. Megan found herself caught in the thick of it, her fear giving way to a fierce determination to survive.

She saw Dre take down an enemy, his movements swift and precise. "Keep moving!" he shouted, his voice a beacon of hope in the madness.

Megan's heart raced as she followed Jerel, her eyes darting around for any sign of danger. She could feel the adrenaline coursing through her veins, her mind focused on one thing: survival.

Suddenly, a figure emerged from the shadows, gun aimed directly at Jerel. Megan's breath caught in her throat as she raised her weapon, her finger squeezing the trigger. The shot rang out, and the attacker fell, his gun clattering to the ground.

Jerel turned, his eyes wide with shock and gratitude. "You saved my life."

Megan's hands shook, the reality of what she'd done sinking in. "We save each other," she whispered, her voice trembling.

Jerel nodded, his resolve hardening. "Let's finish this."

The battle reached its climax as Jerel and his crew pushed into the heart of the factory. The G-Mob fought fiercely, but Jerel's men were relentless. The air was thick with smoke and the scent of gunpowder, the floor littered with the fallen.

Jerel spotted the leader of the G-Mob, a hulking figure with a scar running down his face. Their eyes locked, and Jerel knew this was the moment of reckoning. He advanced, his gun aimed steady.

"It's over," Jerel said, his voice cold and unyielding.

The rival leader sneered, his eyes filled with hatred. "Not yet, it ain't."

They charged at each other, the clash of their bodies echoing through the factory. Fists flew, guns fired, and the air was filled with the sounds of struggle. Megan watched with bated breath, her heart in her throat.

With a final, brutal move, Jerel disarmed his opponent, sending him crashing to the ground. He aimed his gun, his eyes hard. "This is for everyone you've hurt."

The shot rang out, and the rival leader fell, lifeless. The battle was over, but the cost was great.

Jerel's crew emerged victorious, but the price of their victory was steep. Bodies lay scattered, the ground stained with blood. Jerel stood amidst the wreckage, his chest heaving with exhaustion and grief.

Dre approached, his face grim. "We did it, JP. But we lost good men."

Jerel nodded, his eyes filled with sorrow. "I know. But we survived. And we'll honor them by rebuilding stronger than ever."

Megan stepped forward, her heart heavy with the weight of what they'd endured. She took Jerel's hand, her eyes filled with love and determination. "We'll get through this. Together."

Jerel looked at her, his heart swelling with emotion. "Together."

Chapter 18: A New Beginning

The sun was just starting to rise, casting a warm glow over the city as Jerel and Megan packed the last of their belongings into the car. The echoes of their past life in the gritty streets seemed to linger in the air, but there was also a sense of hope, a promise of something new. Jerel took one last look at the warehouse, the place that had seen so much violence and pain, and then turned to Megan.

"You ready for this?" he asked, his voice steady but filled with emotion.

Megan nodded, her eyes reflecting the same mix of sadness and excitement. "Yeah, I'm ready. Let's go."

They got into the car, and as Jerel started the engine, he felt a weight lift off his shoulders. For the first time in years, he was leaving behind the life that had defined him, the life that had almost destroyed him.

The drive to the new city was long, filled with stretches of quiet reflection and moments of shared laughter. They talked about their plans, their hopes for the future, and the challenges they knew they would face. But through it all, their love for each other was a constant, a beacon guiding them toward a better life.

"Starting a business ain't gonna be easy," Jerel said, his eyes focused on the road ahead. "But we got this. We've been through worse."

Megan smiled, reaching over to squeeze his hand. "We got this."

They arrived in their new city as the sun was setting, casting a golden hue over the unfamiliar streets. Their new home was modest but filled with potential, a blank slate for their fresh start. As they unpacked their belongings, the reality of their new life began to sink in.

"This is it," Megan said, looking around the small apartment. "Our new beginning."

Jerel nodded, his eyes shining with determination. "Yeah, it is. And we're gonna make it work."

The first few weeks were a whirlwind of activity. They found a small storefront in a bustling part of the city and began the process of turning it into a legitimate business. It was hard work, but it was honest, and that made all the difference.

Jerel's skills from his past life proved useful in unexpected ways. His ability to negotiate, his understanding of supply chains, and his knack for managing people all came into play as they built their new venture from the ground up. Megan's creativity and organizational skills complemented his perfectly, and together, they made a formidable team.

Their business, a trendy café with a side hustle in urban apparel, quickly gained a following. The locals were drawn to their authenticity, their resilience, and the undeniable chemistry between them. Word spread, and soon, they had regular customers and a growing reputation.

One evening, after closing up shop, Jerel and Megan sat on the rooftop of their building, looking out over the city that had become their new home. The stars were bright, the air filled with the sounds of life and possibility.

"We did it," Megan said softly, her head resting on Jerel's shoulder. "We really did it."

Jerel wrapped his arm around her, his heart swelling with pride and love. "Yeah, we did. And this is just the beginning."

They reflected on their journey, the challenges they had faced, and the love that had carried them through. It hadn't been easy, but they had fought for their happiness, and that made it all the more precious.

"I'm grateful for everything we've been through," Megan said, her voice filled with emotion. "It's made us stronger."

Jerel nodded, his eyes fixed on the horizon. "I wouldn't change a thing. Every moment, every struggle... it brought us here."

They sat in comfortable silence for a while, enjoying the peace that came with knowing they had made it through the worst. Their future was still uncertain, but they were ready to face it together, with all the strength and resilience they had gained from their past.

The days turned into weeks, and their business flourished. They made new friends, built a new community, and found a sense of purpose that had been missing for so long. Jerel's past still lingered in the background, but it no longer defined him. He was a new man, building a new life with the woman he loved.

One afternoon, as they were closing up the café, a young man walked in. He looked around, his eyes wide with admiration. "This place is dope," he said, his voice filled with genuine respect.

Jerel smiled, seeing a bit of his younger self in the boy. "Thanks, man. We've worked hard to get here."

The young man nodded, his eyes shining. "You're an inspiration. Makes me think I can do something good with my life too."

Jerel's heart swelled with pride. "You can. Just keep pushing, no matter what."

As they walked home that evening, Megan looked up at Jerel, her eyes filled with love and pride. "You're changing lives, Jerel. Ours, and others."

Jerel smiled, wrapping his arm around her. "We're doing it together. And I wouldn't have it any other way."

They reached their apartment, the place that had become a symbol of their new beginning. As they stepped inside, the sense of closure and optimism was deeply felt. They had faced the darkness and emerged stronger, ready to embrace whatever the future held. And it looked brighter than they could have imagined.

Don't miss out!

Visit the website below and you can sign up to receive emails whenever Rachael Reed publishes a new book. There's no charge and no obligation.

https://books2read.com/r/B-A-WXARB-QETVD

Did you love *The Virgin and The Kingpin*? Then you should read *Link in Bio*[1] by Rachael Reed!

[2]

Mari's life looks perfect on the 'gram: flawless selfies, glamorous outfits, and makeup tutorials that slay. But behind the scenes, she's barely holding it together. After her fiancé of one year ditched her, Mari's been frontin', keepin' up the facade while her heart's in shambles. With her wedding date approachin' and her followers none the wiser, she decides to bounce on a solo trip to South Florida. She needs a break, a chance to find herself again.

But when she lands, a hurricane hits, throwin' her plans out the window. That's when she meets Jace, a big-time drug dealer who ain't playin' no games. Trapped by the storm, Mari gets a front-row seat to the

---

1. https://books2read.com/u/4XlxB7

2. https://books2read.com/u/4XlxB7

dark, gritty world Jace rules. She's torn between the life she knows and the dangerous allure of Jace's streets.

Mari and Jace's worlds collide in a whirlwind of passion, danger, and secrets. They vibe on a level she never thought possible, but when the storm clears, reality hits hard. Can she return to her old life, or has Jace pulled her in too deep?

What happens on vacation don't always stay on vacation. Back home, the ghosts of their time together haunt them both. Jace's enemies are out for blood, and Mari's online persona begins to crack under the weight of her double life. As threats close in from all sides, Mari must decide if she's willing to risk it all for a man who could be her salvation or her destruction.

"Link in Bio" is a raw, unfiltered dive into the streets where love and loyalty are tested by the grind. This urban fiction novel brings you into the heart of the struggle, with drama, betrayal, and suspense that'll keep you on the edge. From baby mama drama to violent confrontations, Mari's journey is a wild ride through the underbelly of city living. Can love survive the hustle, or will the streets tear them apart?

Dive into this gripping tale of love, danger, and resilience. "Link in Bio" ain't your average love story – it's real, it's raw, and it'll leave you begging for more.

Also by Rachael Reed

Codefendant
Codefendant
Once a Cheater
Once a Cheater
Passport Bro
What Happens in Prison
Preference
Sprinkle Sprinkle
Championship Bad
Street Exodus
Street Exodus
Street Royalty
Pawns of Power
SIS
Cartel Bloodline
Get Money Girls
Skip the Games
Til Death Do Us Part
Backpage Hustle
Link in Bio
The Virgin and The Kingpin

www.ingramcontent.com/pod-product-compliance
Lightning Source LLC
Chambersburg PA
CBHW020507160726

47991CB00007B/2847